WET DREAM

AN EROTIC ADVENTURE

VICTORIA RUSH

VOLUME 8

JADE'S EROTIC ADVENTURES - BOOK 8

COPYRIGHT

Wet Dream © 2018 Victoria Rush

Cover Design © 2018 PhotoMaras

All Rights Reserved

Artificial intelligence never felt so real...

THE
PERSONAL TRAINER

AN EROTIC ADVENTURE

VICTORIA RUSH

Feeling the burn never felt so good...

Everyone's an exhibitionist in disguise...

Jade's EROTIC ADVENTURES

BOOKS 1 - 5

VICTORIA RU

Books 1 -5 in the bestselling series - 60% off

For the uninhibited...

$$\frac{1}{\quad\quad\quad}$$

FEMME FATALE

Reflecting back on the six months since my passionless marriage had ended, I was pleased with how far I'd come. I'd stretched the boundaries of my boring love life with increasingly provocative sexual adventures and explored the different dimensions of my sexuality by opening myself up to new experiences with men and women alike. But I still felt something was missing. I knew that I was attracted to women, but I also liked men. There was something about the act of *penetration* that consumed me.

I think it all started with my first transgender experience with Neve at the Naked Yoga studio. I was surprised how turned on I'd gotten by the sight of a pretty girl with a real cock. I knew she wasn't really a girl, but rather a man who'd been surgically and chemically altered to look like a woman. But it didn't matter. I found the experience of playing with —and being penetrated by—a ladyboy incredibly exciting.

Then there was the mysterious woman on the subway train, who'd fucked me from behind with a strap-on dildo while surrounded by a packed crowd of oblivious rush-hour commuters. I found the experience of being invaded by a real woman somehow even more exhilarating. I envied the power she carried hidden under her business suit and the ability to bring me to new heights of pleasure without even using her hands.

But my obsession with cocks really culminated in my recent fling with the girl next door. I'd found the experience of using a large cucumber to penetrate both of us fascinating. The feel and texture of the vegetable had almost made it feel like a real man's cock. There was something—*organic* about it. No more plastic or silicone toys, this almost felt like the real thing. When I actually fucked Abby with it embedded in both of our pussies, I felt like I was fucking her like a *man*.

Suddenly, inexplicably, I'd become obsessed with dicks. Not being penetrated by one; I was obsessed with *owning* one. To have one of my very own that I could use to fuck any pretty lass that came my way. I wanted the feeling of power that I had over other women where I could violate them, control them, *bolt* them to me.

Which was all the more confusing, because I didn't identify as a butch-type lesbian. I'd never been a tomboy growing up and I liked wearing makeup and dressing up like a girl. And when I had sex with women, I didn't always have to be the one on top. I liked to receive sex from my dominant female partner just as much as give it. So what *was* I exactly? A butch, a femme, a ladyboy wannabee?

One thing I knew for sure was that I was happy in a woman's skin. Going through a sex-change operation was out of the question. I just wanted to know what it would be like to have a real cock, just once. If I could switch roles with a man for a day, a week, maybe even a month, I thought it would be fun. I wanted to see what it would be like to make love to a woman with a real live, throbbing, shooting cock. No more vegetables, no more plastic dildos —the *real* thing.

It had gotten to the point where it was all I could think about. I'd imagine I was a man when I masturbated, putting all manner of artificial phalluses up my pussy and rubbing my hands up and down the shaft imagining myself cumming all over my legs and chest. Lately, my dreams had become increasingly dominated by vivid imagery of my swinging a big dick around, fucking men and women alike. I needed to get this out of my system so I could get back to being a regular, normal, lesbian/bisexual/femme woman. Or whatever I was.

One night before heading to bed, I needed my regular fix. I popped open my computer and went to my favorite ladyboy portal and began watching videos of trannies getting blown and fucking other men and women. It had even gotten to the point where I'd watch animated hentai futanari videos of transgender characters getting it on. At least in the futanari videos, the women came equipped with *all* the lady parts, so I could imagine myself in their role. I wasn't quite ready to get on board with the idea of an *entire* package, with balls and no pussy.

After twenty minutes or so watching the usual videos and playing with myself half-heartedly, I wondered what it would be like to watch a real multi-gender individual having sex. I typed in the search phrase *true hermaphrodites having sex*, and a page opened showing a blonde and a brunette woman dressed in skirts kissing on a bed. At first, they just looked like two regular girls making out. They both had typical soft, feminine features, with high cheekbones, narrow jawlines, and full pouty lips. And they were both *pretty*, with big doe-eyes, long eyelashes, and long, flowing, curly hair. If these were trannies pretending to be women, they were certainly acting the part well.

When they started to disrobe each other, I leaned closer toward the screen. They both had small, natural-looking breasts—full, but slightly floppy and bouncy, like the real things. Neither of them had the hard, round, firm tits that were typical of a surgically-enhanced silicone bosom. And their nipples were soft and plump, with no visible scars. When the brunette pulled the blonde's dress down over her chest and began sucking her teats, I could see them dilate and extend like my own did when they were stimulated. I spread my legs in my nightie and beginning to circle my tingling clit.

Those are no fake boobs.

When they pulled the rest of their clothing off and I saw two large springy dicks point up between their legs, I gasped. Neither of them had balls. Instead, beneath their thick, throbbing cocks they had real women's labia, with a real vaginal opening and a real clit. Best of all, they both had feminine figures, with slender legs and arms, narrow waists, and the distinctive curvature of a real woman's ass and hips.

These were real authentic hermaphrodites! With hard, throbbing cocks. And pussies. And tits. The complete deal!

My fantasy had come to life before my eyes. I didn't have to watch any more cartoon imitations of a true ladyboy. I could now see real live human ones right before my own eyes! When the brunette kneeled between the blonde's legs and took her big dick into her mouth, my juices started pouring down my leg.

Fuck! I cursed out loud. *I want one of those. I want a pretty girl sucking my cock too!*

I flung open my nightstand drawer and pulled out a

large replica cock and balls dildo and began sucking on the end of it like the woman performing fellatio on the video.

Oh, the things I could do if I had a real one of these! I imagined.

The blonde lying on the bed began moaning and throwing her head from side to side, obviously enjoying the other woman's attention. Her cock was thick and hard, pointing straight up from a light mat of blonde pubic hair on her mound. When the camera shifted to a new perspective behind her pelvis, I could suddenly see all of her parts. Her vulva swelled open, revealing her little clit nestled at the vertex of her lips, sitting in sharp contrast to the giant phallus pointing up from her stomach. I wished I could be there sucking her little cock while the brunette sucked her big one.

Imagine—I thought, *a woman actually getting head for a change, instead of giving it!*

I sucked on my fake penis even harder, trying to fathom what that would feel like. My pussy throbbed as I watched the brunette grasp the blonde's cock in her fist and swirl her tongue around the bulbous head like it was a lollypop.

As the blonde began to hump her hips into the other woman's mouth, I mimicked her movement with my own hips. *If I had a cock right now, I'd be humping her face too, getting ready to release my fuel into her.* The camera panned back and forth from a headboard to a footboard perspective, so I could see the reaction of the woman lying on the bed from every angle. Whoever was doing the filming was doing so in a super-professional way, almost like it was a real film. Even the *sound* was ultra realistic, as the blonde urged her partner on with frequent vocal interjections.

"Fuck, yes!" she groaned. "Suck my cock, honey. Feel my wet pussy!"

The camera zoomed between her legs to show her slick labia and inner thighs coated with her lubrication.

God damn, I thought. *This girl has all the working parts.*

As I rubbed my clit between my legs, I sucked on my big silicone cock and squeezed the shaft, practically willing it to come in my mouth. Just when I thought it couldn't get much more intense, the brunette slid further down between the blonde's legs and began licking her pussy. She was eating the blonde out like a champ, licking her up and down her slit then closing her lips over her little bean, sucking and flicking her tongue over her love button.

I watched with fascination as the blonde's cock bounced and bobbed while her lover licked her up and down her snatch. When the brunette placed her hand around the blonde's cock and began jerking it up and down while simultaneously licking her pussy, I placed my dildo on top of my mound and pretended to do the same.

Damn—if only this were a real dick, I thought. *I'd love to know what it feels like to squirt out of my dick all over my belly while having a dual orgasm.*

Suddenly, the blonde placed her hands over the brunette's head and began thrusting her cock into her partner's mouth, and I thought she was going to come.

"Not yet!" I screamed at the computer. "I want to *see* it. I want to see you spurting cum out of that pretty cock of yours!"

The brunette stopped sucking the blonde's cock and stood up at the foot of the bed. She pulled her dress over her head, revealing beautiful round, shapely hips. Then she crawled back onto the bed and lay down beside the blonde, and they switched positions. They looked very much alike, almost to the point that I thought they might be sisters. If it weren't for the difference in hair color, it would have been difficult to tell them apart. When the blonde girl began sucking the brunette's cock, the brunette began moaning, rolling her head from side to side.

Two cocks, two pussies. My mind exploded imagining all the possibilities.

The camera panned back behind the footboard as the blonde leaned forward and pointed her pretty ass up in the air. I could see the familiar V-shaped feminine cleft between her legs. But pointing straight forward from her hole was a hard, thick joystick flapping against her stomach. It was surreal watching the juxtaposition of male and female body parts on the same person. I wanted to fuck her ass with my own cock!

Please God, I pleaded. *Give me a cock for one day. Just one day. I promise to give it back.*

As the brunette writhed and moaned in pleasure from the blowjob she was receiving, the blonde girl on top reached between her legs and began rubbing her own cock. When she shifted lower and placed her hand around the blonde's pole and began jerking it while sucking her pussy simultaneously, I couldn't hold back any longer. I had the first of many powerful orgasms that evening. I came hard grinding the balls of the dildo into my clit as I whacked the shaft like a man. For a moment, I imagined seeing real cum flying out of the cock, as I threw my head back, screaming in passion.

I was intrigued to see if the girls in the video could orgasm more than once like regular women, and I was hoping we'd all come together many times tonight. As the brunette lay on the bed squeezing and playing with her nipples, I wanted to lean over and kiss her sweet face on her lips. The blonde took the brunette's cock back into her mouth, and the camera shifted position behind the head of the woman lying on the bed. The brunette swirled her tongue around the circumference of the blonde's throbbing knob, then plunged her head back down over her cock, impaling it balls-deep right on top of her mound.

Fuck! I thought. *That girl really knows how to give head like a pro.*

I wondered what it would feel like to be deep throated. I'd never been particularly good at giving blowjobs, and when I lifted the dildo off my mound and tried to plunge it deep into my mouth, I gagged.

I suppose that means I'm not a peter puffer at least, I laughed. *I was far more interested in slinging my dick than sucking one.*

When the blonde girl began pinching and twisting her nipples as the brunette sucked her dick, I imitated her. I wanted to be right there with her, owning that dick. Whatever she was doing, I was going to do. For the moment at least, I *was* that dickgirl.

But what they did next absolutely blew my mind. The brunette swung her hips over the blonde's then they both grabbed hold of their poles and began tribbing each other's slits with the heads of their cocks.

I'd never seen tribbing like this before!

The camera panned down over the head of the blonde girl, and I had a full view of her tits and cock framed by the brunette's open vulva while they jerked and rubbed one another's pussies. This had to be the hottest thing I'd ever seen. I was dying to see them spunk their hot sweet cum all over each other's pussies. As I took the end of my dildo and rubbed it against my clit, mimicking the girls, I yelled at my computer screen.

"Cum for me, you hot ladyboys!"

I could feel my orgasm rising within me, and I wanted to see them come all over each other as I came with them.

What could it possibly feel like to cum in two places at the same time? I wondered. *From both your cock and your clit?*

As I rammed the head of my dildo against my mound, I had my second orgasm of the night, shaking my entire body from head to toe. The girls in the video were thrusting themselves harder against one another but still hadn't come. I was beginning to worry that I'd never see them actually come like a man. How they were holding out for this long perplexed me.

I could only guess that the video producers had asked them to take their time to go through all of their ladyboy moves before revealing the 'money shot'. If they were like regular men who could only come once before needing an extended recovery, I was grateful for their strategy. I checked the progress bar at the bottom of the video window. That meant I still had fifteen more minutes of ladyboy action to enjoy!

Suddenly, the brunette lifted herself up and swung her hips over the blonde girl's head then bent over to suck her again. *Now they were sixty-nining each other!* The camera panned back and forth, giving me a glorious view between the legs of each woman as her partner sucked her organ. What a beautiful thing it was to watch a woman's ass and pussy swaying in the air, while another girl sucked her big dick jutting out from her hips!

Why can't everybody be endowed with both sets of sex parts? I thought. *I'm sure many men would enjoy having a pussy as much as a cock. Why can't we all be born as hermaphrodites?*

Just when I thought the two women were finally going to cum, the brunette suddenly shifted her hips lower over the blonde's torso. Then she placed her hand between her own legs and pointed her cock toward the blonde's pussy. The camera panned from head to rear, showing each woman thrusting their cocks into their partner's pussies.

Oh my God! Now they're actually fucking each other! They're fucking and getting fucked at the same time!

I thrust my dildo into my cunt as far as I could and rubbed the firm plastic balls against my clit and came for the third time tonight. I closed my eyes and tried to imagine what it would feel like to have a throbbing cock inside me while I was pumping my own cum inside someone else's snatch at the same time.

"Fuck yessss!" I screamed, imagining I was cumming from both my dick and my pussy.

As the blonde girl lay on the bed squeezing and pinching the brunette's ass cheeks, she pounded her fat cock in and out of the brunette's pussy while they thrashed atop the bed. I was wrong when I thought two hermaphrodites sucking each other off was the ultimate turn-on. This took the act of fucking to an entirely new level.

My pussy spasmed as I watched the two women moaning and humping each other. I could tell from their rapid breathing and contorted faces that they were both getting close to orgasm, and I was hoping they'd finish this way. But with only one minute left in the video, they suddenly pulled out of each other and kneeled facing one another on the bed. Then they grabbed each of their own cocks and began jerking off, watching each other. Within a matter of seconds, they both groaned and squirted white creamy semen all over each other's bellies and dicks.

Typical man-produced porno, I thought. Having the guy pull out at the last second and show his cum. What's the big deal with this whole ejaculation thing, anyhow?

Little did I know, I was soon to find out.

2

RUBBING ONE OUT

I fell asleep that night with visions of futa girls crawling over my body as I sucked, fucked, and played with their ladydicks all night long. It didn't take long for my dreams to turn in this direction, and within minutes I was transported to an ancient Arabian kingdom filled with sorcerers and villains. I dreamt that I was the daughter of a powerful emir, betrothed to the king's son. But I wasn't ready to be married yet, not least because I was secretly carrying on an affair with his pretty daughter Farah.

Farah and I had tried to run away, but she was caught by the palace guards while I escaped to a remote cave in the Arabian desert. After a few days without food and water, I began to explore the large cavern in search of nourishment. I came upon a grotto illuminated by a beam of sunlight shining from a crack in the ceiling. The ray projected onto a gleaming pile of jewels and glazed pottery, sitting beside a gurgling pool of water.

I stumbled toward the pool and began guzzling up the liquid into my parched lips. After I recharged my dehydrated body, I began to sift through the trove. It had obviously been placed to hide someone's riches in a location with an abundant source of hydration. Its keepers would have to travel a long distance over the desert to get here. Surely, they'd have also stored some extra *food* provisions to tide them over on their long journey?

I began to tear off the lids of the assorted containers, desperately looking for anything to eat. The pots and bowls clattered against one another, occasionally breaking into shards, but preserving the integrity of the pretty porcelain-ware was the last thing on my mind. To my dismay, the bowls were only filled with more jewels and coins. The cave probably carried a king's ransom worth of treasure, but that would be of little help to me if I died of starvation in the next few days.

I continued rummaging through the pile until I came upon an odd-shaped jar with a small hole at the top of its tapered end. I picked up the vessel and it was heavier than I expected, which meant it had to be filled with something. The lid to the jar was sealed, so I shook the container to discern its contents. It made a strange rustling sound, suggesting there was something soft inside.

Could it be a grain or nut storage jar? I thought.

I stuck my finger through the hole to see if I could feel what it was, but the contents kept moving around, almost like there was something *alive* inside. I peered through the hole, but there wasn't enough light in the cave to see beyond the curved flute at its end. Thinking it might be a small mouse or some other creature, I banged the vessel against a nearby rock in an attempt to break it open. At this point, I was so hungry I could have eaten just about anything.

But unlike all the other delicate pots and bowls, this vessel wouldn't break. I held the container up into the light to try to read the inscription on its flanks. There had to be something valuable in this flask for it to be fortified so strongly, I thought. The container had a thick coating of soot, so I rubbed my sleeve on its side. Suddenly, I heard a strange rumbling coming from inside the flask as a tendril of smoke began to rise from the hole.

The discharge grew thicker and heavier, and the container began to shake violently in my hands. I looked up at the smoke filling the chamber and gasped as it began to take the shape of a man. He was wearing a large turban and embroidered tunic over puffy trousers. On his feet he wore bejeweled jester slippers. When the apparition began to speak, I almost fainted.

"What is so important," the ghost thundered, "that you've shaken Suleiman the Great from his slumber?"

"I'm sorry..." I stammered, in equal parts frightened and mesmerized by the impressive figure. "I didn't know what was inside..."

"Well, you've awoken the jinni now. What is it that you desire?"

"Jinni?" I said, my eyes widening in wonder. "You mean *genie*? Are you some kind of genie?"

I glanced down at the vessel in my hands and realized it was an oil lamp.

"Are you the genie from Aladdin's Lamp?!" I exclaimed, suddenly excited by my find.

"I don't know who this Aladdin is," the ghost said, "but as the bearer of the lamp, I am beholden to only you. What is it that you wish?"

"You mean you can grant me a *wish*?! Just like in the famous story from Arabian Nights?"

"Yes," the genie said. "*Three* wishes, in fact. So choose wisely. I will return to my cozy home after I've granted your wishes and will not come out again for a hundred years."

"Oh boy!" I said, not hesitating to give it much thought. There was only one thing on my mind right now, and that was my grumbling stomach. "I need food. Lots of food. Enough sustenance to carry me back over the desert to the sultan's palace."

"Your wish is my command," the genie said, raising his arms then snapping his fingers toward the ground beside me.

Suddenly, I was surrounded by piles of fruit, nuts, and dried meat. I grabbed a handful of lamb and rammed it into my mouth, gobbling it down in chunks. As I felt the energy returning to my body, I looked back up at the genie.

"Choose wisely, young lady," he said. "You only have two wishes remaining. That food won't last very long. You might want to ask for something you can enjoy for the rest of your days."

I looked at the genie and paused. I was already surrounded by all the jewels and wealth I could ever possibly need. What else could I use that would bring me additional enjoyment? As I began to feel the nourishment coursing through my veins and reinvigorating my organs, I suddenly smiled.

"I'd like to have a man's cock," I said. "But not just any cock. I want a long, thick one. One that I can cum with repeatedly whenever I want."

"Your wish is my command," the genie said, raising his arms, preparing to deliver my request.

"Wait!" I shouted. "But don't want you to take away my lady parts. I still want to look like a woman, with normal breasts and a pussy and a clit. I just also want to have a fully functioning penis."

The genie paused for a moment as he considered my request.

"I suppose that still counts as one wish," he said. "Not taking anything else away doesn't require any extra effort. Do you have any *other* special requirements for this man penis you dream of?"

Hmm, I thought. *I should be careful he doesn't just give me any old dick.*

I thought about the ones that I'd particularly enjoyed over the years. Then I held up my hand and separated my fingers a few inches.

"I want it to be circumcised," I said. "And straight. Let's say eight inches long, and...*two* inches thick. And nicely upstanding when it's erect. A forty-five-degree angle against my abdomen sounds about right."

"Done."

The genie raised his arms again then flung his hands in my direction. At first, I didn't feel anything, but when I lifted my skirt, I gasped. I had a magnificent, golden-brown, circumcised manhose hanging between my legs! I spread my thighs apart and began to fiddle with my new joystick, and it immediately began to fatten and lengthen. As the phallus began to rise up between my legs, I felt a new kind of tingling between my legs. I watched transfixed as my new member jerked and rose with each new pulse of my heart.

I finally had my very own cock! I thought. *My very own throbbing, bobbing, hard cock!*

I couldn't wait to play with it as I circled my fingers around the shaft and squeezed the hard meat in my hand.

"Um," the genie said, peering at me as I sat dumbfoundedly with my fist around my hard-on. "What would you like for your final wish? I'd like to get back to my peaceful slumber sometime today, if you don't mind."

"Oh, yeah," I said, pausing to contemplate what else I could possibly want.

For a moment, I considered asking him for a playmate, a pretty girl that I could use my new cock on right away. But then I remembered Farah, and I had a better idea. If I was ever going to sneak back into the palace and steal her away, I'd need a pretty good disguise.

"I want you to change my looks a little bit. Just enough so people won't recognize me when they see me. But I still want to look feminine, around my same age, and pretty."

"Your final wish is my command!" the genie said, as he flung his arms in the air then back toward me.

A cloud of smoke rose from my perch in the cave, and I peered over to look in the pool of water to see my reflection. A pretty brunette looked back at me, and I smiled.

This will do just fine, I thought.

Suddenly it occurred to me that I'd need additional resources to steal my beloved Farah away from the clutches of her powerful father.

"Wait!" I called out to the genie. "There's one more thing!"

"I'm sorry," the genie said as he began to shrink and vaporize in the cool cavern air. "You've used up all of your allotted wishes. I wish you well. Now please do me a favor and hide my little lamp so I won't be disturbed for another hundred years."

The smoky apparition began to shrink and collapse, then the swirling cloud of smoke disappeared back into the container. I looked around the cave for a safe place to deposit the lamp, then I pushed a large boulder aside and placed the lamp in a recession behind the rock. If I couldn't use the genie's power for another hundred years, then at least I'd be able to pass it along to my family where I'd hidden him.

As I walked back to the pool of water, I glanced at my

reflection once again. It was strange to see someone other than myself looking back at me, and I ran my hands over my face to be sure it was really me. The girl looking back at me was beautiful with big doe-eyes, high cheekbones, and full pouty lips. As I smiled at my reflection, my penis suddenly started rising up between my legs again.

Apparently, my newly installed manhood *also* found the girl in the water attractive! I pulled off my dress and under-clothes and appraised my full body in the mirrored reflection. I still had nice full, firm breasts and round, shapely hips. I spread my legs and pulled my skin apart. And I still had a pussy—*thank you, Genie!*

I placed my hand over my slit and traced my middle finger up toward the junction of my lips to make sure I still had my clit. As I began to circle it in my familiar way, my eyes widened as my new cock swelled and hardened, and rose in a series of sexy pulsing bobs until it pointed straight up at a forty-five-degree angle.

The genie was true to his word. My cock was truly magnificent. Long, firm, and thick, with a large plum-shaped bulbous head that was already leaking sticky fluid out of its slit. I placed my finger over the opening and swirled it over the viscous fluid, then raised my finger to my mouth.

A little salty—but not disagreeable, I thought.

I couldn't wait to see my cum shoot out of my dick when I had a full orgasm. I placed my fist awkwardly around the shaft and began jerking it like I'd seen so many men do before. I was glued to my reflection as I watched myself masturbate my big cock over the pool. Even though I could feel the pleasurable sensations emanating from my crotch, it still felt like I was watching an entirely different person.

But the feeling coming from my man dick was undeniable. It wasn't all that different from the sensations I felt when I played with my pussy and clit, but it was still...*different*. It felt—*bigger*. I began moaning and grunting as I whacked my big cock, recognizing the pleasure rising up within me, emanating from my hips.

The more I rubbed it, the deeper shade of purple my cock became. The head of my cock was now glistening with a thick coat of sticky translucent fluid. When I placed my hand around the bulb and began to massage the lubrication into my skin, I threw my head back and groaned.

So that's where all the action is, I murmured.

The head of a man's cock was a lot more sensitive than the rest of his organ, just like a woman's clit. All the super-sensitive nerve endings were concentrated in the end. I grasped the base of my organ with my left hand and placed my right hand over the upper half and began jerking myself with two hands.

The feeling emanating from my groin was indescribable. I was just starting to get the hang of this whole jerking off thing, and *two* hands was definitely better than one! As I humped my hips into my hands watching the head of my wet cock pumping in and out of the end of my fist, the strange reflection in the pool peered back at me. As I watched her pretty mouth open in ecstasy, I pounded my cock hard against my mound and moaned in delirious pleasure.

As I began to feel the familiar feeling of an orgasm welling up inside me, I refocused my attention on the tip of my cock as it pistoned in and out of my hands. I didn't want to miss this fireworks show for all the money in the world!

I grunted and groaned as I thrashed my head from side to side, barely able to stand up from the pleasure consuming me. Suddenly, I felt a different kind of sensation, as if I had to pee. Coming from deep inside my perineum, I could feel something pushing to come out. As the crest of my orgasm hit me, I screamed out loud, echoing throughout the grotto.

"Yes!" I screamed. "I'm cumming! I'm cumming from my big, manly cock! Fuck! I'm cummmingggg!"

Suddenly, a thick string of white fluid spurted out the tip of my cock as my pole pulsed repeatedly in my hands. I gasped with each contraction, as a new spurt of white goo squirted out of my joystick, making ripples in the water below. I squeezed my cock so hard between my two hands, I was afraid I might break it. But it just kept throbbing and pulsing in my hands, until the last few spurts of come dribbled from the head. When I finally finished coming, I hunched over, exhausted from the experience of having my first ladyboy orgasm.

That wouldn't be the last of my big dick orgasms today. As the shaft of overhead sunlight drew a wide arc across the wall of my cave, I had five more orgasms before falling fast asleep on my heaping pile of treasure.

But I was more pleased that I'd found a *different* kind of treasure today—the kind that only *I* could spend.

3

———

FUTA GIRL

The next morning, I packed enough food and water to survive the two-day trek through the desert back to Persepolis. I also packed enough jewels and coins to last until I could return to the cave. I hoped to bring Farah back with me, but I knew the king's guards would still be on high alert, and I'd need every enticement possible to steal her away.

Using the rising sun as a navigational aid, I landmarked the location of the cave in relation to nearby mountains, then headed north toward the Mediterranean Sea. I wasn't exactly sure in which direction my home city lay, but I knew that once I reached the coast, I'd have no difficulty finding my way back to the palace. Once I got there, I hoped Farah would somehow recognize me and run away to lead a comfortable life living off the riches I'd found in the cave.

As I trudged through the hot desert sand, I tried to envision Farah's reaction to my new body. We'd often played with improvised dildos in her bedroom, and I was confident that my new mancock would add a fun new dimension to our sex life. As I imagined all the ways I could use my penis to satisfy her, the appendage would swell uncomfortably against my undergarments and I had to stop more than once to relieve the rising passion in my loins. I began to wonder if it had been such a good idea to ask the genie to endow me with an organ with unlimited restorative power. It seemed to have a mind of its own, and once any lascivious thought crossed my mind, there was only one way to calm it down.

By the afternoon of the third day, I'd reached the coast and found myself a day's sail away from the royal capital. I used one of my gold coins to purchase a one-way passage aboard one of the local merchant vessels, then went to the local haberdasher to buy some men's clothes. Beyond the fact that my dress was badly soiled from a week's wandering in the desert, I didn't want to take any chances that my garments might be recognized by the palace guards. Plus, I needed a safe place to store my unruly manhood in case it got any bright ideas to spring another boner in public. Then I checked into a hotel and had a long bath and restful sleep to prepare for my journey ahead.

The next day, I disembarked in the busy port of Persepolis and was glad I'd had the presence of mind to ask the genie to alter my appearance. As the daughter of a prominent emir, I could easily have been recognized by her father's many associates. But with a new identity, I could move around the city with impunity. I considered stopping by my house to inform my family of my change in circumstances but decided it was too risky. My father had already promised me to the king and paid a sizable dowry for my betrothment to the prince. For better or worse, my new identity with my secret riches would have to stay between me and Farah for the time being. In the patriarchal culture of ancient Arabia, my sex enhancement would be scandalous and lead to any manner of negative repercussions.

I approached the royal palace with some trepidation. If my identity were discovered, both Farah and I could be executed for treason. I walked up toward the guard shack outside the palace gates and introduced herself as calmly as possible.

"Good afternoon, sir," I said. "I'm here to see Princess Farah."

"Do you have an appointment?" the guard asked, appraising my masculine wardrobe suspiciously.

"No..." I stammered, "but I'm certain she would want to see me."

"What is your name and your business?"

I hesitated for a moment trying to think of a name to use. I obviously couldn't use my real one, but it had to be something familiar enough to Farah that she'd want to invite her into the palace. I racked my brain for a few seconds, then I remembered the name of Farah's favorite doll from her childhood.

"Tell her it's Jamila," I said. "And that I'm here to deliver a special...*gift*."

"The princess is a very busy royal," the guard said. "You may give me the gift and I will see that she receives it."

I hesitated for a moment, trying to think of a way to gain the guard's confidence.

"This is the kind of gift that is properly exchanged only between...*women*. Tell her that it includes a precious gem. A *green* gem."

The guard looked at me warily, then peered up toward the palace. I knew that he could be punished for breaking royal protocol by allowing unannounced strangers into the palace.

I reached into my purse and pulled out an intricately carved Jade gemstone.

"As you can see, sir, this is a very valuable gem. I'm sure you can understand why I'd like to deliver it to her personally."

The guard looked at the gleaming jewel in my hand, then motioned to another guard.

"Amir," he said to the other guard, "can you escort this young lady to the palace receiving court? She has important business with the princess. Tell her that Jamila is here to see her."

The second guard escorted me to the palace reception room, where I waited for fifteen minutes in the ornate chamber. After fifteen minutes, Farah walked across the marble-floored vestibule to greet me.

"May I help you?" she said. "I don't know anyone by the name of Jamila, but the guard said you had something important to give me."

I desperately wanted to tell Farah who I was, but there were still various palace staffers milling about, and she would have just thought I was crazy. I pulled up my sleeve and showed her the special friendship bracelet that she'd given me many years ago.

"Where did you get this?!" she said, eyeing me suspiciously. "This belongs to a very close friend of mine."

I leaned in closer to Farah so as not to be overheard.

"Princess," I said. "I have information about the whereabouts of your friend, Jade. She asked me to show you this so that we might have a private audience. Is there somewhere we can go to be alone for a few minutes?"

Farah glanced nervously at the palace butler standing on the other side of the foyer, then back toward me. She knew the risks of being found associating with a kidnapping accomplice.

"Come with me to my private chambers," she whispered. "We'll be safe there."

Farah turned to the butler.

"This woman has personal business with me. I don't wish to be disturbed."

"As you wish, your highness," the butler said.

She escorted me into her bedroom antechamber, then closed the door and swung around angrily to face me.

"What do you know of Jade?" she asked. "Is she safe? Where is she hiding?"

I reached out and clasped Farah's hand softly in mine.

"Farah," I said. "It's me, Jade. I've missed you so—"

Farah pulled her hand away and her eyes widened in fright.

"I don't know you," she said. "What kind of trickery is this? What have you done with Jade?"

She looked up toward her door preparing to call for help.

"Guar—" she announced.

I reached over and placed my hand over her mouth and held her close to me.

"Farah," I whispered in her ear. "Just give me one minute to explain. I know things only you and Jade have shared in confidence. It's really me. Remember that time when we were eleven, and we were playing in your big dollhouse? We were playing Mommy and Daddy and you showed me your—"

Farah pulled away from me and gasped.

"How could you possibly know that? Jade would never share such personal confidences—"

"Then we used the little teaspoons to probe our private areas. It was the first time you—"

Farah's eyes opened wide as saucers.

"Oh my God! How could you..."

For the next thirty minutes, I explained to Farah what had happened at the cave, and how the genie had changed my appearance to allow me to get close to her. I shared a few more personal details from our childhood, then she leaned in towards me and ran her hands over my face.

"Jade," she said, as tears streamed down her cheeks. "Is it really you? I was so worried about you. I've thought about you every night..."

I leaned in to kiss her and we wrapped our arms around one another in a passionate embrace. After a few seconds, she pulled away and held my face in her hands as she stared into my eyes.

"It really *is* you! I'd recognize that kiss anywhere. Oh Jade—make love to me again. I've missed your touch..."

Farah pressed her body against mine and we ground our hips together as we kissed passionately. Suddenly, my cock began expanding between my legs, pushing forward in my pants.

Farah pulled away and looked at me with a strange expression.

"What the—?"

"Sit down for a moment," I said. "There's one other thing I haven't mentioned..."

We sat on the edge of her bed, and I finished telling the story, explaining the three wishes I'd asked and been granted by the genie. When I finished, she looked at me dumbfounded.

"Of all the things you could have asked for, why *that*?" she said.

"I don't know," I said, a flush creeping over my cheeks. "I've just been...fantasizing about having one for quite a while. Ever since I played the daddy role in our childhood dress-up games. I thought we might be able to have a little extra fun with it. You know, with you being a virgin and everything—"

"What about all your *other* parts?" she said. "I'd kind of grown attached to you the way you were..."

"Don't worry," I said, caressing Farah's inner thigh. "I made sure to keep all my lady parts. The genie simply gave me a little extra appendage."

Farah reached between my legs and ran her hands over the hard lump in my pants.

"Can I see it?" she asked.

"Of course," I said, unzipping my trousers.

My penis sprung out of my pants and pointed straight up, throbbing quietly between my legs.

"Ohhh!" Farah exclaimed, recoiling in shock when she saw the large organ between my legs. "It's...*enormous*! Does it —work like a regular penis? I'm mean—"

"Yes," I interrupted. "I've been...*testing* it. I assure you, it works just like a regular cock."

"Is a *regular* man's penis this...big?" she asked. "I've never touched one before. Do you mind if I—"

"I thought you'd never ask," I said, leaning in to kiss her.

Farah reached out and clumsily ran her hand over the head of my hard-on and I moaned in her mouth. She pulled away and smiled at me.

"Does it feel good when I touch you like that?"

"Oh yes, sweetie—it feels very good. Please don't stop."

I placed my hand over top of Farah's and guided her to wrap her fingers around my shaft, as I humped my cock in and out of her hands. I began to leak some pre-cum out of my slit and as it ran down the sides of my pole, it became sticky, making it harder for her to slide her hand up and down.

"What's that sticky stuff coming out the top?" she asked. "Is that sperm?"

"I'm not sure, to be honest. The genie didn't give me a man's testicles, so probably not. It must be some other kind of fluid that's a byproduct of the pleasurable feelings."

Farah rolled her fingers together, feeling the gummy substance.

"It's getting a bit sticky down there. Let me clean you up and see if we can make this more enjoyable for you."

Farah went into her washroom and emerged with a moist towel and some jars of colored liquid in her hands. Then she knelt down on the floor between my legs and wrapped the moist towel around my organ and rubbed it up and down a few times to remove the sticky fluid from the head and the shaft.

"Maybe this will make it a little more comfortable," she said, pouring some lemon-scented oil from one of the jars into her palm then rubbing her hands together. Then she placed both of her hands around the shaft of my cock and began pulling the skin up and down.

"Oh God," I moaned. "That feels so good, Farah. Rub my cock and make me feel good. I dreamed of you doing this to me for several nights."

The feeling of the warm oil on my cock magnified the plea-surable sensations several fold. I cursed myself for not trying this earlier, as I'd only jerked my jock with the dry skin of my hand. But now it felt like I imagined a wet pussy would feel, and as Farah jerked me softly, I closed my eyes hoping I'd soon have her sweet honeypot embracing my throbbing member.

As the pleasurable feelings escalated within me, I began to thrust my hips harder and faster into Farah's hands, moaning and grunting in delight. Before long, I was forcing her hands far enough up to graze her mouth, and she stopped and smiled at me devilishly.

"You know those rumors we heard about what some women do to a man's cock to *really* make him feel good? Have you fantasized about *that* too?"

"Yes," I panted, pushing the tip of my cock closer to her mouth.

Farah lowered her head and began to swirl her tongue around the head of my pole, and I threw my head back and groaned.

"Yes, Farah," I panted. "Lick my cock. Suck me like a lollipop."

Farah lowered her mouth and circled her lips around my bulb and began sucking on it like a popsicle. I'd never felt anything so good before, and I whimpered in ecstatic pleasure.

"That feels so good, baby," I moaned. "Suck my cock like a lollypop. Does it taste good?"

"Mmmm," Farah hummed, as she continued sucking the head of my dick.

She placed her two hands around the shaft of my dick and pistoned it between her fists as she sucked on the head. I began to feel the familiar sensation I'd experienced over the last few days just before I shooted cum.

"Oh baby," I groaned to Farah, "you're going to make me cum. I'm going to cum soon. Make me cum, Farah!"

Recognizing I was nearing the peak of my pleasure, Farah increased the speed of her motions as she squeezed my shaft tightly between her two hands. When she began flicking her tongue on the underside of my cockhead, I threw my head back and screamed as I felt my cum racing up inside me.

"Farah!" I screamed. "I'm cumming baby! I'm cumming in your mouth!"

Farah's eyes widened as she felt my cream filling her mouth and she pulled off me as we both watched the spurts of cum shoot out the end of my cock in long streams of white goo. She watched my face contorting in agony as my chest heaved with each new pulse of cum spurting from my dick. When I finally stopped, she climbed on the bed beside me and we both fell back on the mattress.

"Did you like that, Jade?" she said. "Do you like your new boy dick?"

I turned my head toward her and pulled her face into mine, tasting my salty cream in her mouth as I kissed her passionately.

"Yes," I panted. "I've grown quite attached to it over the past few days. But *this* was something altogether different. It feels a whole lot better when someone *else* is playing with it."

Farah smiled at me coyly.

"Do you like the way I play with it? Was I good for my first time?"

"Yes," I said, lying on my back, exhaling heavily. "It was *mine* too. That was the first time I've ever gotten *head* that particular way."

Farah glanced between my legs and noticed that my cock hadn't lost any of its firmness and was still bobbing over my stomach with each new heartbeat.

"I think there's a *lot* of things we can try for the first time with that joystick of yours. I've got a few ideas—"

Farah suddenly rolled over on top of me and spread her legs apart, gripping my cock between her thighs.

"I bet there's a few *other* places that big snake of yours hasn't explored yet"

I placed my hands beside Farah's head and pulled her toward me, penetrating her mouth with my tongue. I had indeed dreamed of exploring other parts of her with my newfound love muscle. We quickly pulled our clothes off one another, and after a few moments reacquainting herself with my lady parts, she kneeled over my hips and reached between my legs to point my cock into her hole. As she dragged it back and forth across her wet slit, we both moaned, peering into each other's eyes. Then she slowly lowered herself over my flagstaff, savoring every inch as it sunk deeper and deeper into her fiery canyon.

"Oh my God, Jade," she said when my cock had fully penetrated her chamber. "That feels *way* better than the pickles and eggplant we used to experiment with. It's so warm! I can actually feel you throbbing inside me!"

"Uhnnn," I groaned, soaking up from the incredible sensation radiating around my hips. "I never imagined it would feel this good. Fuck me, Farah. Fuck me with your sweet pussy."

As Farah began to rock her hips over me, grinding her mound against mine, we both gasped.

"Oh, Jade!" Farah groaned. "Fuck me with your man cock. Fill me up and pound me with your big love muscle. I want to feel you cum inside me."

As we rocked our hips together, I watched Farah's face as her mouth opened wider and wider and her moans grew louder and louder. I grabbed the side of her hips with my two hands and pulled her back and forth over me as I thrust my cock deep inside her. Within a few minutes, her eyelids began to flutter and her eyes rolled back and she let out an otherworldly groan.

"Uhnnn—Jade!" she panted. "I feel it. It's happening. I'm going to cum all over your pretty cock. Cum with me baby! I want to feel you spurting inside me. Oh God, Jade, I'm cummminggggg!"

Farah grunted and groaned as her body spasmed wildly on top of me, thrashing and heaving as she screamed my name. Within seconds, I felt the cum rising within me and my cock began pulsing in rhythmic spurts inside her. I squeezed her hips tightly in my fists as we locked our bodies together in simultaneous orgasm.

When our mutual contractions finally stopped, Farah collapsed on top of me and we rubbed our sweaty tits together as I held her impaled to my hard cock still throbbing inside her.

Farah lifted her head off my shoulder and smiled at me.

"I'm *glad* you wasted one of your wishes on this," she said. "I can't imagine a more loving gift that you could have brought me upon your return."

I kissed her softly as one last spurt of cum spilled into her sweet, warm pussy.

4

A PRINCELY MATTER

Farah and I made love many more times over the course of the day, then we made plans to steal away over cover of darkness that evening. We decided the safest strategy was for me to leave the palace so as not to invite extra suspicion, then for her to meet me at the docks where we'd bribe our way aboard another shipping vessel. Then we'd backtrack our way to the cave and sneak aboard another ship headed toward Europe. With our newfound riches, we could hide away the rest of our days in relative luxury.

Farah bade me farewell on the front steps of the palace, then I headed down the trail in the direction of the port. But as I approached the woods surrounding the castle, someone grabbed my sleeve and pulled me into the thicket. It was Crown Prince Ali, Farah's brother. He dragged me behind a tree and pinned my arms over my head on the trunk.

"What business did you have visiting my sister?" he asked, glaring at me.

I was worried that he'd somehow discovered my identity. If he knew I was his runaway bride, I'd never be able to escape his clutches. But if he couldn't identify who I was, there'd be no reason to detain me any further. All I had to do was remain calm and stick to my story.

"I...was simply bringing her a gift I'd made for her as a loyal follower."

"What *kind* of gift?" Ali said, eyeing me suspiciously. "The guard said it included some precious stones."

He looked at my modest commoner's clothes, paying particular attention to the swelling of my breasts in my tight bodice.

"You don't look like the kind of person who can afford to give away something like that away. And why are you wearing a *man's* clothes? What are you trying to hide?"

"Nothing," I stammered. "I just find them more...comfortable. A woman can't be too careful on such a windy day about protecting her modesty when the slightest breeze might reveal more than our customs dictate."

Ali looked at my long pants, squinting at the crotch area.

"What is your name and your family lineage that you can afford such lavish gifts?"

"My name's Jamila," I said, trying to think of a common surname to maintain my cover. "My father is a jeweler by the name of Khalil Khan."

"I've never heard of this jeweler," the Prince said. "The royal family knows most of the goldsmiths in town. There's something about your story that doesn't ring true."

I racked my brain trying to think of another reason for visiting the princess.

"We thought bringing a gift to showcase our wares might curry favor with the royal family. It's hard to make inroads in such a competitive bus—"

"Liar!" Ali said, pressing my wrists against the rough bark. "I overheard you and my sister doing much more than exchanging *jewelry* in her room. What business does a woman dressed in man's clothes have trying to seduce the princess?"

Ali thrust his hand between my legs and squeezed my crotch, suggesting that only a man should have the right to court his sister. But he stepped back when he felt the unusual lump on my mound.

"What the hell?!" he said, his eyes flying open in confusion.

He grabbed my pant legs with both hands and flung my trousers to the ground. My half-erect cock sprang forward and bobbed between my legs. Ali's dark brooding eyes and his forceful manner pressing me against the tree had apparently awoken another kind of primal urge within me.

He stepped forward and tore off my shirt, then pulled my bodice up, revealing my bouncing tits on my chest.

"What kind of...*person* are you?" he exclaimed, spending more time ogling my rapidly growing boner than my pretty girl tits.

"I...was born with both sets of reproductive organs," I lied. "Please don't tell anyone. If anyone else knew of my deformity, I'd be shunned from our community. I meant no harm to your sister—"

"You were *fucking* my sister? With *that*?!" He brought his gaze back up to my plump breasts. His pupils were wide as saucers, and I could tell he was excited by the strangely attractive transgender person before him. "How *can* you—if you're a woman?"

"I guess you'd say I was neither a man nor a woman," I said. "I'm a...*hermaphrodite*, with both sets of functioning sex organs."

He stepped back a few feet to appraise my full body, then squinted between my legs. He reached forward and ran his fingers over my rapidly dampening hole. Then he stepped back again and shook his head in disbelief. But the tenting in the front of his trousers betrayed his true interest in my ladyboy body.

He glanced at his moist hand and twitched his middle and forefinger in a feigned fingering action.

"Does *that* work too?" he asked, looking at my pussy.

I began to realize this might be the perfect opportunity to deflect his suspicions about my plans with his sister.

"Yes," I smiled. "Would you like to try?"

Ali hesitated for a moment, then he stepped forward and placed his hands over my breasts. He squeezed and pinched them for a moment to be sure they were real, then he put his right hand between my legs and thrust his fingers inside my snatch. I swayed my hips to his motion and moaned, as my cock pressed against his stomach. He leaned in to kiss me and I pushed my hips toward him, feeling his equally hard member trapped in his pants. I lowered my hands and began unbuckling his trousers, then reached inside to grasp his swollen dick. He removed his fingers from my pussy and we began to masturbate each other as we moaned in each other's mouths.

After a few minutes, he pulled back to look more closely at my cock and I pulled his trousers all the way down to the ground. We were now facing each other our poles pointing straight out toward one another. I stepped forward and play-fully slapped my hard-on against his as if jesting with swords. My cock was almost twice as large as his, and I enjoyed my little moment of dominance over him.

I bet this wasn't the way you envisioned fucking your new bride, I thought, as a sneer began to spread across my face.

I could tell Ali was enjoying our little cockplay, and the head of his member was soon coated in a thick film of pre-cum. I kneeled between his legs on the soft ground and took his organ into my mouth. I was surprised how much of it I could take into my mouth, since his erection couldn't have been much more than four inches long. I sucked on his head and reached between his legs to play with his balls, and Ali groaned as he thrust his cock in and out of my mouth. Before long, his balls rose tighter against the base of his cock and I knew that he'd soon release his spunk. With one final thrust, he grabbed my head with two hands and pulled my face down onto his bush as he squirted his cum inside me.

Typical alpha male, I thought. *Showing he can have his way with women any way he desires.*

But I had my *own* ideas for demonstrating who was in charge in this relationship.

After Ali finished cumming in my mouth, I stood up and smiled at him then I grabbed my big hard-on with both hands I began to wank it, moaning seductively. He feigned disinterest as he began to button up his trousers, but when I lifted one leg and showed him my glistening pussy, he paused. While I jerked the shaft of my cock with one hand, I reached between my legs and finger-fucked myself with the other. Ali had obviously never even dreamed of such a scenario (these being the days long before online video or even the printing press), and he stood there with his mouth agape as he watched me jerk and jill myself in double pleasure. His cock began to rise again, and before long it was bobbing straight out from his open trousers.

"Do you *want* some of this?" I said, glancing between my legs. "I bet you've never fucked a ladyboy before, have you?"

Ali quickly pulled his trousers back down and pushed me back against the tree. He grabbed the end of his dick and pointed it toward my hole, then thrust himself forward, ramming his penis inside me. This was the first time I'd been fucked by another cock in my altered state, and even though Ali's was smaller than most of the other ones I'd had, it was an agreeable feeling. As I felt the familiar pleasurable sensations building up inside me, I rocked my hips in synchronicity with him while he thumped me against the hard bark of the tree.

As he fucked me, Ali kept staring at my hard cock bobbing between our torsos. It was a deep purple color now and glistening with pre-cum all over the head. I reached down and encircled it with my hands and began jerking it up and down as Ali thrust his own cock in and out of my pussy. He began to moan loudly, and I knew he was about to cum. I sped up the pace of my jerking action, and just as he grunted one last guttural moan, I spurted a thick stream of cum up between our abdomens, landing a big glob on his face. Ali pulled out of me and lurched backwards as he wiped the sticky fluid from his face, spreading it over the sides of his hips.

"Did you enjoy that, my prince?" I smiled. "There's much more of that whenever you want it," I lied. I just needed to give him enough motivation to keep me alive until Farah and I made our escape.

"Perhaps we can meet here again tomorrow?" I said.

"Yes," Ali said, still fixated on my dick. Unlike his rapidly detumescing member, mine was still pointing straight up on my belly, bobbing and pulsing as hard as ever. As he continued staring at it, I saw new life in his little flute as it began to thicken and rise.

"Would you like to touch it again?" I said, motioning to my giant erection.

Ali paused for a moment, looking around the woods to make sure we were alone. Then he stepped forward and touched the head of my dick tentatively. I didn't know if he was more captivated by the unusual *size* of it, or the simple fact that he was touching another man's hard-on for the first time. Either way, his own cock quickly rose to its previous excited state, and I could tell he was turned on touching my cock. As he began to jerk my shaft, he wrapped his fingers around his own member, and awkwardly tried to jerk both of us off with two separate hands. After a few minutes, he became frustrated trying to coordinate the ambidextrous actions, and he pressed his hips forward until our dicks touched.

Then he placed the underbelly of his erection against mine and wrapped his two hands around both of our joined cocks. As he began to hump his hips against mine, his little pecker disappeared in his hands while my much larger organ thrust a full four inches above the top of his palm. Ali seemed to be getting worked up by the sight of our two cocks frotting one another and before long, he came again with three anemic spurts landing on top of my cock. The feeling of his watery semen lubricating my cock was enough to put me over the edge, and I squirted another series of long ropes onto his chest as I came for the second time.

As Ali maintained his grip on our joined cocks, rubbing the wet heads of our throbbing members together, I saw him unconsciously lick his lips.

"That was lovely, my prince," I said. "But something tells me you're not done feasting on my body. Would you like to see what a lady cock *tastes* like?"

Ali paused for a moment looking at me uncertainly, then he glanced around the wood again nervously.

"It's okay," I said. "This will just be our little secret. I've never done this with another *man* before. You make me feel like a real ladyboy."

I could tell Ali liked me talking dirty to him as his cock twitched and dribbled as I spoke to him.

"Come, my prince. Let me feel your lips around my big manly cock. Make me feel like a real ladyboy."

Ali stepped forward tentatively and placed his hand over my throbbing dick. It throbbed in his hand and I leaned in to kiss him, plunging my tongue into his mouth, signaling l that I wanted something *else* in his mouth. He slowly lowered himself until he was kneeling between my legs, then he pressed his lips forward to touch the head of my cock. My cock pulsed, and a thin dribble of pre-cum squirted onto his tongue. He paused for a moment, unsure whether he wanted to continue, then he plunged my cock deep into his cavity.

For someone who pretends to be a virile heterosexual, I thought, *he sure knows how to suck a cock.*

I moaned in pleasure as he grasped my shaft with two hands and swirled his tongue around the head, bobbing up and down over me. Seeing his little dick bouncing between his legs as he consumed my python, I decided to give him some of his own medicine. I placed my hands behind the back of his head and began thrusting my big pole deeper into his mouth. His expert cocksucking technique was having its desired effect and I soon began to feel my cum welling up inside me.

"Fuck, yes, Prince!" I panted. "Suck my big cock! I'm going to dump my cum down your throat. Here it comes!" I yelled. "I'm cumming!"

I pulled Ali's head as far as I could toward my belly and thrust my dick against his throat. He gagged for a moment, then relaxed as I filled his mouth with my seed. My cock pulsed for many long seconds, with each contraction pouring more semen into his mouth. Eventually, it overflowed and began spilling out the sides, dribbling down his cheeks and neck. When I finally finished spasming in his mouth, he pulled his head back and stared at my twitching eye, winking at him as it spilled out the last vestiges of my spunk.

I glanced between his legs and saw that his penis had returned to its previous excited state and smiled at him.

"I think maybe the prince isn't quite finished with me," I said. "Was there anything *else* you wanted to play with before we go our separate ways?"

Ali stood up and grabbed my tits angrily in his two hands.

"You're a very dirty girl, Jamila," he sneered. "But I like it. We will have to do this again very soon."

As he pressed his body up against me one last time and thrust his tongue into my mouth, I reached around behind his hips and squeezed his butt cheeks. He began to grind his cock against mine again, moaning into my mouth as we frotted for a few seconds. When I reached under his cheeks and pressed my finger against his anus, he grunted approvingly. I rubbed my cock harder against him, then slowly inserted my middle finger into his hole. As he titled his hips back toward me accepting me into his private space, I felt his dick pulse against mine.

"Do you like that, my prince?" I said.

Ali pinched my nipples firmly and moaned in my mouth. I began to turn my body slowly around, tracing a line with my dripping cockhead over the side of his hips as I kissed his neck while fingering his anus. When I got directly behind him, I placed my dick between his thighs and dry-humped him, prodding his balls with the head of my dick. Ali moaned approvingly, and I removed my finger and placed the head of my cock over his opening.

Now we'll really see who's the alpha male in this relationship, I thought to myself. *It looks like we'll both be losing our virginity today.*

By fucking him up the ass, I felt a certain measure of revenge for his attempting to steal me away from my beloved Farah. Besides, this was something I hadn't yet tried with my new ladyboy cock, and I always wondered what it felt like when two men did it. The tip of my cock was already wet from my previous cum, and the head slipped into his opening surprisingly easily. But it was definitely tighter than his sister's pussy—*much* tighter. I pushed further into his ass, feeling the warmth surround my thick organ. I wasn't sure how far I'd be able to penetrate him, and I was surprised when my mound pressed against his ass cheeks.

As I began to thrust my firehose inside him, Ali groaned and whimpered in pleasure. There was something about the idea of fucking a man with my lady cock that I found particularly pleasing. Maybe it was just the utter *filthiness* of it, or maybe it was the fact that I was dominating the second most powerful man in the kingdom. Either way, I enjoyed it immensely, and before long I could feel my orgasm preparing to boil over.

But just as I was about to deposit my load into his bowels, we heard a strange rustling sound coming from the side of the wood about twenty feet away. We both looked in the direction of the sound and saw a herdsman peering at us from behind a tree. I didn't know how long he'd been watching us, but the recognition that we'd been spotted raised my passion even more.

I grasped Ali's flanks with my two hands and pulled his ass firmly against me as I thrust my cock deeper into his ass.

"I'm coming, your majesty!" I screamed, for the whole wood to hear. "I'm cumming up your tight little ass!"

I held the prince tightly to me as I pulled him toward me with each contraction of my pole. As my semen spurted into his tight canal, his opening made a rude hissing sound.

I hoped the would-be spy would soon spread the truth about our tiny-dicked, ladyboy-loving prince. Something told me there'd be no more betrothals for the young prince anytime in his future. After I pulled my steaming cock out of Ali's ass, he quickly pulled up his pants and scurried up the hill in the direction of the palace.

That's right—run, you wannabe. Soon there'll be no heirs remaining in the kingdom to carry on the royal lineage. When the king finds out about your little dalliance in the woods with the ladyboy, there'll be two offspring banished from the palace.

5

———

RUDE AWAKENING

I awoke the next morning in a cold sweat in my regular bed. I looked around the room for a moment to reassure myself that I was actually in my own home and no longer in my Arabian dream. There was a giant spot on the sheets under my hips and I reached between my legs half-hoping to still find my throbbing cock still attached to me. Alas, I only had my usual slippery, but still tingling, soft slit.

Fuck, that was a hot dream! I thought. *But where did all that violent man-fucking come from?*

I was more confused than ever about my sexual identity and predilections. But one thing I knew for certain. I was horny as hell from all the ladyboy imagery in my extended dream, and right now I just needed satisfaction. I reached over into my nightstand drawer and pulled out my big fake cock replica and shoved it into my steaming honeypot. As I came over and over again screaming Farah's name, I imagined it was me fucking her.

I'm definitely going to have to experiment with this ladyboy thing some more, I thought, as I squirted yet another orgasm onto my wet sheets.

Artificial intelligence never felt so real...

THE
PERSONAL TRAINER

Feeling the burn never felt so good...

Everyone's an exhibitionist in disguise...

Jade's

EROTIC

ADVENTURES

BOOKS 1 - 5

VICTORIA RUSH

Books 1 -5 in the bestselling series - 60% off

THE HABIT - PREVIEW

OBSESSION

For the rest of that day, I couldn't shake the pretty nun from my thoughts. It wasn't just her celestial beauty—there was something about her veiled appearance that got me worked up. Now that I knew she had sexual feelings, my mind raced with a million questions.

Was this the first time she'd acted on her impulses? Did she masturbate frequently in the privacy of her own room? Or had she simply gotten turned on watching me play with myself? Did she come to the library often for this express purpose? Was this her only safe outlet for expressing her sexuality? If so, why did she choose to live such a sheltered life, if she harbored such strong earthly desires?

But mostly, I just obsessed about what she *looked* like under all her formal vestments. As soon as I got home, I tore off my clothes and imagined our bodies bending together in every possible position. I imagined sucking her and licking her and fucking her, making her come in every possible way I could conjure. I fantasized about making her moan and scream in ecstasy, as I worshipped every square inch of her gorgeous body.

After I came for about the tenth time that day, I lay in my bed exhausted and naked, thinking about how I might see her again. Searching for her at the local abbey was out of the question. They probably wouldn't even allow me to *talk* with her, and if so, it would only be through the front gate for a limited time. And my chances of running into her elsewhere in the Chicago area were practically nil. For all I knew, the library may have been the only sanctioned area outside the convent that she was allowed to visit.

My only chance for seeing her again was at the library. I knew that today's encounter might just have been a lucky happenstance, but I hoped that our silent tryst had awoken a primal urge within her that she'd want to revisit. My only hope was that she'd return to the library again soon and that this time we'd have a chance to connect on a more personal level. If so, I had no intention of letting her slip through my fingers again. At the very least, I hoped we could have a coffee together to give me a chance to get to know her a little better. I fell asleep that night imagining her lying beside me, our bodies intertwined, her skin still dewy from making love to me all day long.

<hr>

The following morning, I headed out early to be at the library for opening time. I didn't want to take any chance that I might miss my blue-eyed nun if she had the same idea as me. If I had to stay there all day every day for a month, I was ready to do whatever it took. I packed my laptop to work on client projects in case she didn't show up, but if she did, I planned to be ready. I wore a mid-thigh skirt and my favorite cream-colored silk blouse, with absolutely nothing on underneath. As I walked up the front steps of the library, feeling the cool morning breeze wafting up against my bare pussy, my nipples hardened, producing two protrusions in my blouse.

If she wants more of this, I thought, *I'll really give her a show today.*

When the library opened, I searched every floor and every corner of the facility, but the nun was nowhere to be found. I hadn't expected to see her right away, so I found an open table near the chair where she'd sat yesterday and flipped open my computer. But as much as I tried to concentrate on my work, I kept glancing over at the vacant chair, thinking about what had happened yesterday.

I glanced around the room to make sure no one could see my computer screen, then I typed in the search phrase *videos of nuns having sex*. I paused before hitting the Enter key, then added the word *lesbian*. I didn't want any men polluting my fantasy. A video titled *Confessions of a Sinful Nun* popped up. I clicked the pause button, then inserted my headphones into the audio jack so I'd be able to listen to the video privately. The video was different from most other pornos, with top-quality cinematography, multiple attractive characters, and a real forty-minute story arc.

This should distract me for a while, I thought.

The video began with the mother superior at a convent informing a young nun that two other nuns had missed communion, asking her to search the surrounding grounds for them. The pretty nun headed out along a trail in the woods, and after a few minutes heard the sound of two women giggling in a sheltered glade. She peered through the branches and saw the two nuns fondling each other under their habits. It didn't take long for them to remove most of their clothing, until they were wearing nothing but white stockings.

As one of the nuns lay on the ground, the other one straddled her face, grinding her bush into the nun's mouth. While she humped the girls face, she turned her body and began fingering the other nun's pussy. Before long, the nun on top began to shake, as her breasts quivered on her chest. "Oh yes!" she said, pulling the other girl's head tighter against her pussy. "Right there!" Just as she came on the other girl's face, the mother superior suddenly walked up behind the pretty nun and asked her if she'd seen anything. The other girls overheard the conversation and quickly scampered away, while the third nun covered for them.

If convent life is anything like this, I thought, *no wonder my blue-eyed nun felt the need to travel so far afield to escape the overprotective clutches of her abbey.*

The video was part of an extended series, and as I watched each clip, I fingered myself quietly under my desk. For over an hour, I took myself to the edge of climax, slowly backing down each time. I wanted to save myself for my *own* special nun if she came back. But when one of the scenes introduced a sister resembling the one I saw yesterday, I couldn't hold back any longer. I was just about to cum when a familiar black and white figure emerged from the stacks about twenty feet away.

It was the same blue-eyed nun from yesterday!

She walked directly past my desk looking straight ahead, carrying another book under her arm. She sat in the same chair as yesterday and opened the book on her lap, then peered up over the binding in my direction. Her eyes widened when she recognized me, then she quickly crossed her legs and directed her attention back to her book. I glanced at the chair I sat in yesterday and was disappointed to see that it was now occupied. But from my vantage point just a little further away, I actually had a more direct view of the nun. And from her seated position directly in front of me, she had a clear view of knees and skirt at crotch level.

This could actually work out better than I expected, I thought.

But as the nun kept her head buried in her book, feigning disinterest, I began to wonder if we'd crossed signals.

Had I frightened her away yesterday with my bold overture? If so, why hadn't she just gotten up and moved to a location where I wouldn't be such a distraction?

When her foot started bobbing again on her knee, her intention became clearer.

What a sly fox. She's signaling her interest in me through her body language.

I closed my computer lid to give her an unobstructed view of my upper body, then unbuttoned two buttons on my blouse to reveal my cleavage. As my breasts pressed firmly against the silk fabric, I could feel my nipples hardening once again. The nun looked up from her book and did a doubletake, before directing her attention back down toward her book.

"Yes," I whispered under my breath. "Did you like that? Give me a little more of your attention, and I'll *really* give you a show."

The nun had her head down, but I could see her long eyelashes fluttering in excitement against her brow. I knew she must have been torn between her vow of celibacy and her desire to engage me more directly.

She just needs a little more incentive, I thought.

I shifted position in my chair and spread my legs two feet apart. A few seconds later, she peered up, and I wobbled my knees under the table to redirect her focus. When her eyes dipped under my desk, they widened in shock when she saw my bare pussy exposed under my skirt. This time, she didn't look away.

As I spread my knees further apart, she stared straight into the junction of my thighs. I reached under the table with my right hand and hiked my skirt up a few more inches. She now had a clear, unobstructed view of my bare, glistening pussy. She froze for a moment, staring between my legs, then peered down again into her book, as a flush fell over her cheeks.

I smiled, knowing how conflicted she must have been between her pact with God and the tug of raging hormones racing through her system. There was something about the frustration she was experiencing that made this even more of a turn on. I looked around the room to make sure no one else was looking, then I placed my fingers over my clit and began to circle it slowly.

If she looks up again, I'll make it impossible for her to turn away this time.

I squeaked my chair, and within a few seconds, the nun's eyelashes lifted above her book again. When she saw my hand between my legs, her leg straightened over her knee and her book wobbled on her lap. As I placed my hand over my vulva and began to rub it over my slit, I could feel my juices spilling out of my pussy, coating my thighs and ass. The feeling emanating from between my legs was sublime, magnified all the more knowing my pretty nun was getting just as wet as me under her heavy habit.

As I began to feel my passion rising, my mouth opened unconsciously, and seeing the look of unadorned pleasure on my face, the nun's lips parted also. Recognizing that we'd made sustained eye contact for the first time, I felt an electric charge go through me, and I pressed my fingers tighter against my snatch. I could have come at any moment, but I wanted to savor this for as long as I could.

When her eyes dipped back under my table, I slipped my middle fingers into my opening and began to fuck myself as my two outer fingers slid up and down the inside of my thighs. I wanted to bring my other hand under the table to massage my clit directly, but it was too dangerous. It would have been far too suspicious for any onlookers to see a woman squirming in her library chair with two hands pumping under the table.

Instead, I pressed the palm of my hand against my mound and shimmied my hand up and down over my button while I pressed my two fingers as deep as I could into my hole. The nun was now bouncing her eyes up and down between my face, my bouncing tits, and my cavitating legs under the table. Her foot began bobbing more rapidly on her knee and I could see the front of her frock rising and falling as she breathed heavily.

For the first time, I could make out the bulge of her breasts under her gown, and although they were heavily concealed by all the layers of fabric, I could tell she had a plump set of tits. As I fantasized about sucking on them, I increased the pace of my finger-fucking and spread my legs wider, until they were almost a full one hundred and eighty degrees apart.

As my orgasm began rising within me, my mouth gaped open and I nodded, indicating that I was about to cum, and the nun did the same. Whether she was feeling the same sensations under her robe, or was simply mirroring my expression in sympathy with me, I wasn't sure. When my climax finally poured over me, I thrust my hand hard against my mound and clamped down over my fingers.

As the pretty nun watched the look of ecstasy wash over my face, I pressed back against my chair and sat shaking in a spastic seizure for a full thirty seconds. When my contractions finally abated, I sat up in my chair with my fingers still embedded in my pussy, savoring the heightened sensitivity inside my warm cavern.

When I finally regained my senses, I realized that I'd been so lost in my own pleasure that I'd temporarily lost focus on what the nun was doing. I wasn't sure if she'd managed to rub one out herself, or if she had just been concentrating on enjoying my show. But when she uncrossed her legs and spread her knees apart, her plan soon became apparent. A few moments later, her right hand disappeared from the edge of her book and I noticed some movement under her gown in the area between her legs as the textbook in her lap begin to shake.

Clever girl! It looked like she'd cut a hole in the side of her frock so she could have direct access to her private areas.

The movement under her gown began to take on a familiar and steady pattern as she began to squirm in her seat. Our eyes met once again, and her lips parted as her chest began to rise and fall more rapidly.

Fuck! I thought. *She's actually going to let me watch her come this time!*

I pushed my fingers harder into my pussy and began shimmying my palm against my clit again. But this time, I paced myself so I could cum with her. As her movements under her robe increased in intensity, I sped up my movements in kind. We were staring directly into each other's eyes now, and I could tell she was getting close.

When she nodded her head to me signaling that she was about to cum, I couldn't stop myself from moaning as my second climax took hold of me. The nun's thighs pulled together as she hunched forward in obvious climax, and I gushed all over my hand as the contractions inside my pussy sprayed my love juices all over my thighs and ass. I clenched my face trying to stifle my moans, but a few pitiful whimpers escaped. At this point, I didn't even care if anybody noticed what I was doing. I was on my own special wavelength with the pretty nun across the aisle, and for now at least, we were the only two people in the room.

After a few seconds, the nun's body relaxed and she lay back against her chair. The book resting on her lap popped up as she pulled her hand from between her legs, then she smiled at me softly and closed her eyes, laying her head on the backrest. I looked around the room to make sure no one else had witnessed our silent affair, then I pulled my sopping fingers out of my cunny and cleaned them with some wet wipes in my purse.

There was no way I was going to leave the library alone today without at least talking to the pretty nun. When she stood up from her chair ten minutes later and walked toward the stacks to return her library book, I quickly collected my belongings and followed her. A dribble of lubrication run down the inside of my thigh as my pussy pulsed in excitement, knowing I was about to have my first real contact with the blue-eyed beauty.

Read More

ABOUT THE AUTHOR

If you would like to receive notification of new book(s) in Jade's Erotic Adventures, follow me at http://bookbub.com/authors/victoria-rush.

If you have a moment, please post a brief review on my Amazon book page at mybook.to/wd . Even just a couple of sentences will help other readers find and enjoy this book as much as you hopefully did.

Follow, share, like, and comment at:

www.facebook.com/authorvictoriarush
www.pinterest.com/authorvictoriarush
www.twitter.com/authorvictoriarush
authorvictoriarush@outlook.com

Hope to see you again soon!